WORLD WAR II

The Child's World®

Published by The Child's World®
1980 Lookout Drive • Mankato, MN 56003-1705
800-599-READ • www.childsworld.com

ACKNOWLEDGMENTS
The Child's World®: Mary Berendes, Publishing Director
Red Line Editorial: Editorial direction
The Design Lab: Design
Amnet: Production
Content Consultant: Rev. Arthur Wheeler, Associate Professor of History, University of Portland

Photographs ©: Joe Rosenthal/AP Images, cover; The Design Lab, 5 U.S. Signal Corps/AP Images, 7; Bettmann/Corbis, 8; Corbis, 9, 12, 18; Harris & Ewing/Library of Congress, 10; Library of Congress, 13 (top), 13 (bottom), 14, 16, 17; Elias Goldensky/Library of Congress, 15; United States Coast Guard, 21; United States Army, 22; dpa/Corbis, 24; U.S. Marine Corps/Library of Congress, 27; United States Army Air Forces/Library of Congress, 28

Design Elements: Shutterstock Images

ISBN 9781631437090
LCCN 2014945407

Printed in the United States of America
Mankato, MN
November, 2014
PA02243

ABOUT THE AUTHOR

Thomas K. Adamson has written dozens of nonfiction books for kids on sports, space, history, math, and more. He lives in Sioux Falls, South Dakota, with his wife and two sons. He enjoys sports, card games, and reading and playing ball with his sons.

TABLE OF CONTENTS

CHAPTER 1   **INVASION** **4**

CHAPTER 2   **WAR BEGINS** **8**

CHAPTER 3   **END OF THE WAR**

            IN EUROPE **20**

CHAPTER 4   **END OF THE WAR**

            IN THE PACIFIC **26**

★ ★ ★

TIMELINE 30

GLOSSARY. 31

TO LEARN MORE 32

INDEX 32

CHAPTER ONE

INVASION

★ ★ ★

I t was 3:00 a.m. on June 6, 1944. Thirty-one-year-old Bernard Feinberg got on a boat. Feinberg was from New Jersey. He had volunteered to join the U.S. military in 1940. He was now part of a huge invasion.

Germany had invaded Poland in 1939. The United Kingdom and France declared war. Then Germany attacked France in 1940. Feinberg and thousands of other soldiers were going across the English Channel to take it back. On June 6, 1944, the United Kingdom, the United States, and the other Allies were part of the largest invasion by water in history. It was called D-day.

The water of the English Channel was choppy. Most men got seasick. U.S. ships fired onto the beaches. American and British planes flew overhead. They were going to France to bomb targets there.

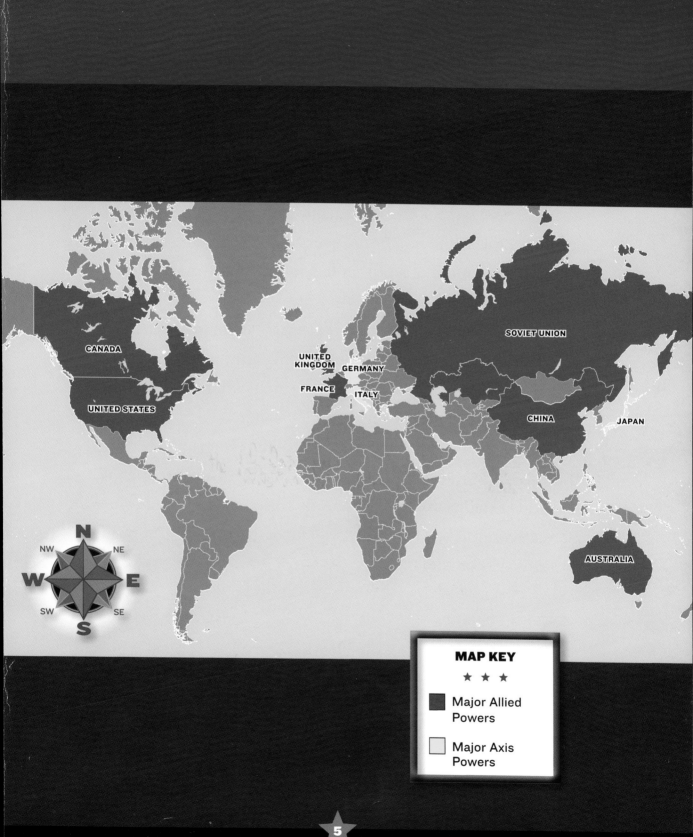

CANADA

UNITED STATES

UNITED
KINGDOM
FRANCE
GERMANY
ITALY

SOVIET UNION

CHINA

JAPAN

AUSTRALIA

NW   N   NE
W   E
SW   S   SE

MAP KEY

★ ★ ★

Major Allied
Powers

Major Axis
Powers

The Germans were surprised by the size of the invading force. But they regrouped quickly. They returned fire furiously.

Feinberg's boat approached shore just after 6:00 a.m. The soldiers waded waist deep in the water. They rushed to the beach. There were already dead and wounded soldiers all around. Bullets and bombs fell everywhere. Feinberg's unit reached the bottom of a hill on the beach. There they found some protection.

Around noon, American tanks began to come ashore. Feinberg and his group went up the hill. They were still under gunfire. Now Feinberg saw dead German soldiers. He also saw many German soldiers being taken prisoner.

Feinberg looked back at the beach. Thousands more soldiers were landing. More planes flew overhead. American and Allied soldiers would eventually free France from the German army. The D-day invasion made the Allied victory in World War II possible.

U.S. troops arrive on the beaches of Normandy during the second day of the D-day invasion on June 7, 1944.

ANOTHER VIEW

Try to imagine how it would feel to be on the beaches on D-day. It seems like you can't go onto the land because of all the gunfire and bombs. You see your fellow soldiers running up the hills and inland. Would their bravery help you feel brave too?

CHAPTER TWO

WAR BEGINS

★ ★ ★

Benito Mussolini

The Allies defeated Germany and the Central Powers in World War I in 1918. The Treaty of Versailles ended that war. This agreement prevented Germany from having weapons or a military. It also forced Germany to pay **reparations** to the Allies for damages done during the war. Germany's economy suffered after the war.

Adolf Hitler and his Nazi Party wanted to make Germany a prosperous military power again. Hitler became the leader of Germany in 1933.

Benito Mussolini took power in Italy in 1922. He believed in ruling the country with total control. This was called fascism. Anyone who disagreed with the government was punished.

Adolf Hitler was a charismatic speaker who won many Germans over to the Nazi cause with the passion of his speeches.

Meanwhile in Japan, military leaders wanted to extend Japan's reach and influence. Japan invaded China in September 1931. Japanese soldiers killed and tortured hundreds of thousands of people.

Italy, Germany, and Japan each wanted to expand their country's territory and power. They formed an **alliance**. They became known as the Axis Powers.

People in Washington, D.C., read news of Germany's invasion of Poland.

Hitler wanted to take over more land for Germans to live in. He believed the so-called **Aryan** race was superior to other races.

Hitler **annexed** Austria in 1938. The Austrians did not put up a fight. Hitler created a new Nazi government in Austria. Next, Germany took over Czechoslovakia.

Hitler then turned to Poland. Germany invaded on September 1, 1939. Germany used 250,000 troops and 1,600 planes. The planes bombed Polish cities with a tactic called **blitzkrieg**. The lightning-fast invasion showed the world Germany's military strength. The Soviet Union invaded Poland along with Germany. No country was able to help Poland militarily. The United Kingdom and France declared war against Germany on September 3. World War II had begun.

On May 10, 1940, Germany invaded Holland and Belgium. It took only days for Germany to overtake the two small countries. The Germans surrounded British and French forces at Dunkirk in France, near the Belgian border. The Allies retreated across the English Channel.

The German army then swept through the rest of France. It entered Paris on June 14. Germany occupied much of France until the D-day invasion in 1944.

With France out of the way, Germany launched a massive air attack against the United Kingdom between June and October in 1940. The German air force, called the Luftwaffe, bombed British airfields, ports, and cities. British planes battled the Luftwaffe in the air. The British air force shot down hundreds of German planes. Germany eventually gave up the Battle of Britain after months with little progress.

Hitler thought that if Germany defeated the Soviet Union, the United Kingdom would be forced to give up. It would

British and French troops evacuate France at Dunkirk as German forces close in.

have no allies remaining. Hitler also felt that the Soviet Union was growing too powerful. He didn't trust the Soviet Union's leader, Joseph Stalin.

London suffered frequent air raids during the Battle of Britain.

The Germans and Soviets had signed a deal before the war not to attack each other. The Nazis broke this deal. Three million German soldiers invaded the Soviet Union starting on June 22, 1941. Germany attacked toward Moscow, Leningrad, and the grain-growing region of the

Joseph Stalin

The United States shipped bombers and other weapons to the Allies under the Lend-Lease Act.

Ukraine. The Soviet Union refused to be defeated despite the huge attacks.

The Germans attacked again the following year and fought the momentous Battle of Stalingrad. The Battle of Stalingrad lasted from July 1942 to February 1943. The German invasion resulted in millions of **casualties**.

Most Americans did not want to send soldiers to another European war in 1939. It would cost too much money and too many lives. They wanted to remain **neutral**.

But U.S. President Franklin Roosevelt wanted to help the Allies. In 1941, Roosevelt suggested the Lend-Lease Act. This law allowed the United States to sell weapons to the United Kingdom. The United Kingdom would not have to pay for them until later. Next, the United States stopped selling iron and oil to Japan. The United States was looking less neutral all the time.

Franklin Delano Roosevelt

The U.S. had a large naval base at Pearl Harbor, Hawaii. Japan believed the only thing stopping it from taking more territory in the Pacific was the U.S. naval fleet. Japan launched a massive surprise attack on Pearl Harbor on December 7, 1941, to destroy the fleet.

Approximately 360 Japanese aircraft took off from aircraft carriers 275 miles (443 km) north of Hawaii. The bombers and fighters swept over Pearl Harbor in two waves. The attack lasted less than two hours. More than 2,500 Americans were killed. The Japanese attack damaged or destroyed 18 American ships and nearly 300 airplanes.

The U.S. Congress declared war on Japan the next day. Germany and Italy soon declared war on the United States. Americans were now in a world war again.

The U.S.S. *Shaw* burns in Pearl Harbor after the Japanese surprise attack.

A Japanese bomber swoops toward the devastated Pearl Harbor.

Six months after Pearl Harbor, the U.S. Navy proved that it was not defeated. On June 3, 1942, Japan bombed the U.S. air base on Midway Island, approximately 1,000 miles (1,600 km) from Hawaii. The Japanese planes returned to their aircraft carriers.

The U.S.S. *Yorktown* took a hit from Japanese bombers and eventually sank during the Battle of Midway.

DETENTION CAMPS

After the Pearl Harbor attack, many Americans feared that Japanese Americans would hurt the war effort. Two months after Pearl Harbor, approximately 110,000 Japanese Americans were put on trains and sent to detention camps. Barbed wire and armed guards surrounded the camps. Guards had instructions to shoot anyone who tried to leave. The camps closed in January 1945. Many Japanese Americans returned to their homes to find strangers living in them.

The U.S. planes then took off from their aircraft carriers. They attacked the Japanese planes when they were refueling. The Japanese planes couldn't take off while refueling and were easy targets. The Americans destroyed four Japanese aircraft carriers and more than 300 planes. The American victory at Midway put the Japanese navy on the defensive.

ANOTHER VIEW

At the start of the war, few women in the United States worked in what were traditionally considered "men's jobs." These included factory jobs in the aircraft industry and with weapons manufacturers. But the men leaving to fight in the war left those positions empty. Approximately 6.5 million women went to work to fill those jobs. Posters of "Rosie the Riveter" encouraged women to work in factories. Women also worked on farms, drove trucks, and made weapons. But after the war, returning soldiers who had served their country expected their old jobs back. How would you react to being fired from a job you had done well for years so a veteran could have his job back?

CHAPTER THREE

END OF THE WAR IN EUROPE

★ ★ ★

Thanks to the entrance of the United States, the Allies were gaining momentum in Europe. In early 1944, the Allies prepared for the D-day invasion. Allied planes attacked German plane factories and oil refineries. The Allies shot down hundreds of defending Luftwaffe planes. This relentless attack all but wiped out the German air force threat. Allied planes destroyed railroads and bridges in northern France. This prevented the German army from moving easily.

The Allies invaded France on June 6, 1944. More than 5,000 ships and 11,000 planes crossed the English Channel overnight.

The massive D-day invasion allowed the Allies to land a huge amount of supplies in France in the following days and weeks.

At least 156,000 men and 50,000 vehicles had landed in Normandy, France, by midnight on June 6. Approximately 4,900 Allied soldiers were killed, wounded, or missing on the first day of the D-day invasion. One million men had landed within weeks. Two million men and 500,000 vehicles were part of the huge invasion over the next three months.

The invasion was successful. But difficult fighting was still ahead. The Allies now had to move across France and into

U.S. tanks advance through heavy fog during the Battle of the Bulge.

Germany. Throughout the rest of 1944, they fought steadily toward Germany's capital, Berlin.

It took many months, but the Allies drove the German army out of France and back toward Germany. In December 1944, Germany launched a surprise attack across the German border into Belgium. Two hundred and fifty thousand troops and 600 tanks attacked American lines.

American defenses broke down right away. The Germans rolled into Belgium. The German advance made a bulge in the American line.

American planes could not defend the American ground soldiers because of foggy weather.

PARATROOPERS

Soldiers called paratroopers had one of the most dangerous jobs in the war. They jumped from planes and landed behind enemy lines using parachutes. Some blew up bridges. Others took control of landing fields.

Greatly outnumbered, the Allies fought against the German tanks with grenades and bazookas.

The weather finally cleared on December 23. Ten thousand American planes attacked the German army. The planes also dropped supplies to the American army. The Battle of the Bulge was over by the end of January 1945.

The battle was costly for both sides. For the Americans, 19,000 were killed, 47,000 wounded, and 15,000 captured. Germany suffered more than 100,000 killed or wounded.

TUSKEGEE AIRMEN

Black men were trained as pilots starting in 1941. Racist attitudes held by much of the American public had kept blacks from becoming pilots before. The airmen trained at a segregated base in Tuskegee, Alabama. Their main job was to escort bombers. They made sure the heavy bombers made it to their targets and safely back to base. Tuskegee Airmen shot down 108 enemy planes. They didn't lose a single plane that they were protecting. They proved that black pilots were equal in ability to white pilots.

By 1942, the world was learning about what came to be known as the Holocaust. Hitler and the Nazis had rounded up millions of Jews and other minorities and murdered them. Those killed included Polish people, Jehovah's Witnesses, homosexuals, political enemies, and others who didn't fit the Nazi's racist Aryan ideal. Hitler had a special hatred for

Prisoners at the concentration camp in Dachau in southern Germany celebrate as U.S. troops arrive to liberate the camps on April 30, 1945.

Jewish people. He also blamed them unfairly for Germany's loss in World War I.

The Nazis brought the prisoners to concentration camps such as Auschwitz in Poland. Prisoners were forced to do hard labor. They didn't get enough food. Many died of starvation and overwork. Those who were unable to work, including pregnant women, children, the elderly, and the sick, were killed in gas chambers.

The Nazis murdered at least 6 million people in the Holocaust. The Allies liberated the camps as they advanced through Germany. The atrocities they saw in the camps and the sickly condition of the survivors shocked the world.

Allied forces reached Berlin, Germany, in April 1945. Soviet Union soldiers found Hitler's remains in Berlin. He had killed himself.

Germany officially surrendered on May 8. This date is now known as V-E Day, for Victory in Europe.

ANOTHER VIEW

Imagine you lived in France during World War II. You know that the Nazis are rounding up Jews. You are not Jewish but your neighbors are. You have a room in your house they could hide in. If they are discovered the Nazis could kill your family and target others in your community. Would you risk your family's safety to protect your neighbors?

CHAPTER FOUR

END OF THE WAR IN THE PACIFIC

★ ★ ★

Meanwhile, the Allies were preparing for an invasion of Japan. They needed an air base closer to Japan. U.S. Marines invaded the tiny island of Iwo Jima on February 19, 1945. Taking the island was slow, deadly work. The Japanese had nowhere to retreat. They fought to the death. The fighting on Iwo Jima finally ended in March.

The Allies needed to take the island of Okinawa to stage an invasion of Japan. Okinawa is more than 900 miles (1448 km) south of Tokyo, Japan's capital. The island had 110,000 Japanese defenders. They fought from caves and bunkers.

U.S. Marines prepare to storm Iwo Jima on February 19, 1945.

The battle on Okinawa was by some measures the hardest fighting of the entire war. The United States launched attack after attack throughout May. Japanese suicide airplane pilots, called kamikazes, crashed into U.S. ships and killed many. On June 21, the United States finally won the battle. More than 12,500 U.S. soldiers died. More than 100,000 Okinawan civilians also died.

U.S. military leaders did not want to invade Japan. They feared more of the hard fighting they had faced on Okinawa and Iwo Jima. They wanted a quicker way to end the war.

The atomic bombs dropped on Hiroshima and Nagasaki (pictured) caused huge amounts of death and devastation but helped bring the war to an end.

NAVAJO CODE-TALKERS

Navajo Code-Talkers helped win the war in the Pacific. They used the Navajo language to send secret messages. Very few people outside the Navajo tribe knew the language. They used this code to send messages about the location of the enemy. It was a quick and safe communication method. The Japanese could never break the code.

Scientists had been working on a new kind of bomb since 1939. The atomic bomb, or A-bomb, could cause incredible destruction. The A-bomb was ready by summer 1945.

The Allies sent Japan a message demanding that it surrender. Japan would not.

On August 6, a plane called the *Enola Gay* dropped the A-bomb over Hiroshima, Japan. The bomb exploded 1,900 feet (580 m) above the ground. It destroyed the city in a blinding flash. A mushroom cloud rose into the air.

The bomb was a terrible success. It flattened the city. More than 70,000 people died instantly. Tens of thousands more died due to **radiation** poisoning over the following years.

The Allies warned Japan again to surrender or there would be more destruction. Japanese leaders didn't respond. The United States dropped another A-bomb on August 9 on Nagasaki. It killed between 60,000 and 80,000 people. Japan finally surrendered five days later on August 14.

The deadliest war in history was finally over. At least 60 million people had died in the war around the world. More than 400,000 Americans were killed.

World War II was a war many in the United States did not want to fight at first. But after Pearl Harbor the United States fought hard. The Allies put the atrocities committed by the Nazis and the Japanese to an end.

ANOTHER VIEW

Harry Truman became president of the United States in 1945. He soon had a big decision to make. Dropping the A-bomb would kill tens of thousands of Japanese, but it would end the war quickly. A U.S. invasion of Japan would take longer and cost many American lives. What choice would you have made if you were president?

TIMELINE

September 1931	Japan invades China.
September 1, 1939	Germany and the Soviet Union invade Poland.
May 1940	Germany invades Holland, Belgium, and France.
June–October 1940	German planes bomb British targets in the Battle of Britain.
June 22, 1941	Germany invades the Soviet Union.
December 7, 1941	The Japanese navy launches a surprise attack on Pearl Harbor.
June 1942	The Battle of Midway turns the tide of the war in the Pacific.
June 6, 1944	The Allies carry out the D-day invasion at Normandy, France.
December 1944– January 1945	The Germans fail to push the Allies out of German-occupied territory in the Battle of the Bulge.
February–March 1945	Both sides sustain heavy casualties during the Battle of Okinawa.
May 8, 1945	Germany surrenders to the Allies.
August 6, 1945	The United States drops an A-bomb on Hiroshima, Japan.
August 9, 1945	The United States drops an A-bomb on Nagasaki, Japan.
August 14, 1945	Japan surrenders to the United States.

GLOSSARY

alliance (uh-LYE-uhns) An alliance is a partnership between two countries in a war. Germany and Italy had an alliance in World War II.

annexed (an-EKSD) A country or territory that has been annexed has been taken control of by another country. Hitler annexed Austria in 1938.

Aryan (AIR-ee-uhn) In Hitler's un-scientific understanding, the Aryan race consisted of white, non-Jewish people from northern, central, and western Europe. Hitler believed in Aryan superiority to other races.

blitzkrieg (BLITS-kreeg) Blitzkrieg means "lightning war." Blitzkrieg was a quick and massive attack the Germans used to invade countries, led by their air force and masses of tanks.

casualties (KAZH-oo-uhl-teez) Casualties are soldiers who are wounded, captured, missing, or killed in war. Many battles in World War II had massive amounts of casualties.

neutral (NOO-truhl) A neutral country does not support either side in a war. Many Americans wanted the country to remain neutral in World War II.

radiation (ray-dee-AY-shuhn) Radiation is the flow of particles of atoms that is sent out from something that is radioactive. Radiation from the atomic bombs dropped on Japan harmed people's health for years after the bombing.

reparations (rep-uh-RAY-shuhnz) Reparations are compensation paid in money and goods by the losing countries in a war to the winning countries. Germany was forced to pay reparations to the Allies after World War I.

TO LEARN MORE

BOOKS

Callery, Sean. *World War II.* New York: Scholastic, 2013.

Sandler, Martin W. *Why Did the Whole World Go to War?: and Other Questions about World War II.* New York: Sterling Children's Books, 2013.

WEB SITES

Visit our Web site for links about World War II: **childsworld.com/links**

Note to Parents, Teachers, and Librarians: We routinely verify our Web links to make sure they are safe and active sites. So encourage your readers to check them out!

INDEX

atomic bomb, 28
Axis Powers, 9

Belgium, 10, 22
Berlin, 22, 25
blitzkrieg, 10
Britain, Battle of, 11
Bulge, Battle of the, 22–23

D-day, 4, 6, 10, 20–21
Dunkirk, 10

English Channel, 4, 10, 20

fascism, 8
Feinberg, Bernard, 4, 6
France, 4, 6, 10–11, 20–22, 25

Hiroshima, 28
Hitler, Adolf, 8, 10–12, 23, 25
Holocaust, 23–25

Italy, 8–9, 17
Iwo Jima, 26–27

kamikazes, 27

Lend-Lease Act, 14
Luftwaffe, 11, 20

Midway, Battle of, 17–19
Mussolini, Benito, 8

Nagasaki, 29
Nazis, 8, 10, 13, 23–25, 29

Okinawa, 26–27

Pearl Harbor, 14–18, 29
Poland, 4, 10, 24

Roosevelt, Franklin
    Delano, 14

Soviet Union, 10–13, 25
Stalin, Joseph, 12
Stalingrad, Battle of, 13

United Kingdom, 4, 10–11, 14